Stephanie Stansbie • Polona Lovsin

WHAT'S THAT NOISE, LiTTLE MOUSE?

A PRESS-THE-PAGE NOISY BOOK!

LITTLE TIGER PRESS

London

The moon was up, the night was still and Little Mouse
was half asleep. All at once, there came a noise –
a long and loud and trembling sound . . .

"What's **that**?" cried Mouse, now wide awake,
holding his covers tight. But then he heard
another noise, a steady tapping in the night . . .

Tick - tock!
Tick - tock!

Tick - tock!

Little Mouse crept out of bed and tiptoed from his room.
His heart was all a-flutter!

Outside, the wind was stirring in the trees,
shaking the leaves with a shivering breeze.
Through the hall window, crisp and clear,
came a bustling,

rustling,

whispering sound . . .

Ssssssssssssshhhhh

"Oh my goodness!" Little Mouse gasped,
and he scampered downstairs
as fast as he could!

ıhhhhhhhhhh!

Standing alone in the kitchen,
he couldn't believe his ears . . .

a wet and wobbly
dripping noise dribbled
in the dark . . .

Drip!
Drip!
Drip!

"It's a ghosty!"
Little Mouse cried,
and he ran and hid
in the cupboard.

The moonlight crept through the cupboard door, casting shadows all around. Little Mouse heard a grating sound – a creaking, squeaking, scraping sound . . .

Crrrreeeeeeaaaak!

"The ghosty's coming to get me!"
Little Mouse wailed.

He raced up the stairs and dived beneath
the covers. But then there came the
worst noise of all . . .

a rattling, chattering, clattering sound – and it was heading straight towards Little Mouse . . .

Shaking and quaking, and quivering and shivering, Little Mouse let out the loudest sound of all . . .

hhhhaaaaaahhhhhhhhh!

Quick as a flash, Mummy Mouse scampered into the room.

"What is it, little one?" she called.

"A g-g-ghosty!" Little Mouse cried. "It's louder than loud. Can you hear it?"

"I can hear Owly singing his song," said Mummy Mouse.

Too-whoo! Too-whoo!

"And your little clock ticking to lull you to sleep."

Tick-tock! Tick-tock! Tick-tock!

Sssssshhhhhhhhhhhhhh!

"There's a breeze in the trees, wishing you good night,"

"a kitchen tap dripping,"

Drip! Drip! Drip!

"a cupboard door creaking,"

Crreeeeeeeaaaak!

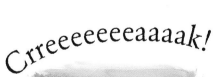

"and your window pane rattling."

Rattle! Rattle! Rattle!

Mummy Mouse smiled . . .

"No ghosty, then," said Little Mouse. "I didn't think there was."
Mummy Mouse tucked him up and cuddled him close.
"Sweet dreams, sleep tight, wish-a-mouse a quiet night!"
she sang to him softly.

And soon the only noise to be heard in
the whole of the house . . .

was the **thunderous** sound of a little mouse snoring!

Snoorre!

Snooorre!

Ssssnnoooorrrre!